Words to Know Before You Read

Let's Learn The **Mm** Sound

mammoth motorcycle

many mouse

map movie

masks mumbles

monkey mummies

monster museum

moon mystery

more

www.rourkeeducationalmedia.com

Edited by Precious McKenzie
Illustrated by Marc Mones
Art Direction and Page Layout by Tara Raymo
Cover Design by Renee Brady

Library of Congress PCN Data

The Museum Mystery / Meg Greve
ISBN 978-1-62169-250-8 (hard cover) (alk. paper)
ISBN 978-1-62169-208-9 (soft cover)
Library of Congress Control Number: 2012952746

Rourke Educational Media
Printed in the United States of America,
North Mankato, Minnesota

rourkeeducationalmedia.com
customerservice@rourkeeducationalmedia.com • PO Box 643328 Vero Beach, Florida 32964

The Museum Mystery

Counselor
Lou

Counselor
Nico

Will

Marcos

Viv

Rosie

Written By Meg Greve
Illustrated By Marc Mones

"We're off to the museum," calls Counselor Lou.

"I want to see a movie," mutters Marcos.

"Here we go!" says Counselor Nico.

"Move over motorcycle! Move over moped! Move over motorbike!" chant the children as the bus rumbles along.

"What a mixed up ride. We are here!" says Counselor Lou.

"I want to see the moon rocks!" yells Will.

"I want to see the map," says Rosie.

"Where is the men's room?" mumbles Marcos.

Rosie says, "Great! The museum has many masks. Let's go see!"

The group marches off to see the many masks.

There are monkey masks, mouse masks, monster masks, and...

13

"Oh no! A missing mask!" yells Rosie.

"Let's go look for it," says Viv.

The children look around the mummies.

They look through the moon rocks.

They look under the wooly mammoth.

Counselor Lou says, "This is a mystery. The mask is really missing."

"What is that?" yells Viv.

"It's a monster!" screams Rosie.

"It's a monkey!" cries Will.

It isn't any of those things.

"It's Marcos!" yell the children.

"This was more fun than a movie!" giggles Marcos.

After Reading Word Study

Picture Glossary

Directions: Look at each picture and read the definition. Write a list of all of the words you know that start with the same sound as *missing*. Remember to look in the book for more words.

 **map** (MAP): A map is a plan of an area that shows the area's main features.

 **masks** (MASKSS): Masks are coverings worn over faces to hide the faces.

monkey (MUHNG-kee): A monkey is a small ape.

monster (MON-stur): A monster is a large, scary creature.

motorcycle (MOH-tur-sye-kuhl): A motorcycle is a heavy vehicle with two wheels and an engine.

mummies (MUH-meez): Mummies are dead bodies wrapped tightly in cloth to preserve the bodies over a long time.

About the Author

Meg Greve lives in Chicago with her husband and her two kids named Madison and William. They love to go see the mummies, masks, and moon rocks at the museum!

Ask The Author!
www.rem4students.com

About the Illustrator

Marc Mones is a Spanish illustrator. He lives in Bolvir, a small town in the Pyrenees, with his wife Rose, his two sons Gerard and Martin, and his four cats. Marc has liked to draw since he was a little kid. His father is also an illustrator and his mother is a very good painter. His very favorite things to draw are monsters!